THE BREMEN TOWN
MUSICIANS

AND OTHER ANIMAL TALES FROM GRIMM

THE BREMEN TOWN
MUSICIANS

AND OTHER ANIMAL TALES FROM GRIMM

Retold by Doris Orgel
Illustrated by Bert Kitchen

A NEAL PORTER BOOK
ROARING BROOK PRESS
BROOKFIELD, CONNECTICUT

Text copyright © 2004 by Doris Orgel
Illustrations copyright © 2004 by Bert Kitchen
Published by Roaring Brook Press
Roaring Brook Press is a division of Holtzbrinck Publishing Holdings Limited Partnership
2 Old New Milford Road, Brookfield, Connecticut 06804

Distributed in Canada by H. B. Fenn and Company Ltd.

Library of Congress Cataloging-in-Publication Data
Orgel, Doris.
The Bremen town musicians and other animal tales from Grimm / retold
by Doris Orgel ; illustrated by Bert Kitchen.— 1st ed.
p. cm.
"A Neal Porter Book"
ISBN 1-59643-010-9
[1. Animals—Folklore. 2. Folklore—Germany.]   I. Grimm, Jacob,
1785-1863.   II. Grimm, Wilhelm, 1786-1859.   III. Kitchen, Bert, ill.   IV. Title.
PZ8.1.O59Br 2003
398.2′0943′0452—dc21
2003008989

Roaring Brook Press books are available for special promotions and premiums.
For details contact: Director of Special Markets, Holtzbrinck Publishers.

First edition 2004
Printed in the United States of America
2 4 6 8 10 9 7 5 3 1

—CONTENTS—

— A Note from The Reteller —

I always loved tales about animals, especialy the funny, clever ones in my old tattered, dog-eared Grimm. I've long been searching for a book of these tales, in English, to share with my children and now with my grandchildren. Maybe no such book existed. In any case, I couldn't find one. So I started these retellings—which, luckily, became this book, with illustrations that outdo my fondest hopes.

I have a favorite memory that goes way back. It's of my father enacting *King of the Birds*, making a wide range of realistic, raucous noises, and flapping invisible wings. I also remember my serious, studious mother reading *The Hare and the Hedgehog*, in *plattdeutsch*, as the Grimms retold it, and somehow she was able to make that quaint, peculiar-sounding dialect intelligible to me.

My language as a child was German. We lived in Vienna, Austria until 1938. We fled when Hitler came. Since then my language has been English. My home is in America. I seldom miss my native land, or things I left behind.

But I still love the German language.

I worked directly from the German text, retelling these tales, all but *The Hare and the Hedgehog*. To do right by that one, I had to work from *plattdeutsch*, which was hard, but fun.

My aim was to stay true, if not always to the letter, then to the spirit of the Brothers Grimm. Naturally, I tried to make my version fresh, appealing to readers today. This meant making a few changes, skipping what seemed preachy or obscure, but always very carefully, so as not to harm the "oldness," because that's where the magic is.

Putting both my languages to use, I did my best to share in English what delighted me in German, and I trust that children here and now will be delighted too.

—*Doris Orgel*

—A Note from The Illustrator—

I think that there is in me and I suspect always will be, a large proportion of "child." At least I hope so, for I believe it is that element which allows us, as adults, to continue seeing things in that innocent way we used to as children, in those far off days when life and the whole world seemed so full of mystery. Then it seemed there were boundless possibilities, as we explored and felt our way through each new experience, filing it into that other part of us we call memory. Sounds, smells and particular situations can each remind us of past events, some happy and not so happy. As the Grimm Brothers say: "Truly, that is the way of the world," when, for example, the Cat eats his friend and partner, the Mouse—in that case not so happy.

Very rarely in the history of children's literature have there been writers who have been able to present situations and encase ideas that have remained so meaningful and symbolic to us, as readers, in this strange and wonderful world, sometimes presented through people, sometime in the guise of animals.

It is a rare gift. We have to go back as far as 57 B.C. to find Aesop, still popular today, and from then forward to around 1800 A.D. to locate Jacob and Wilhelm Grimm who can still hold our attention.

Although they were far apart in time, somehow I think of Aesop and the Grimm Brothers for like Aesop, the Grimm Brothers have that very special ability to appeal to children and to the "child" in all of us.

—*Bert Kitchen*

THE BREMEN TOWN MUSICIANS

A MAN HAD A DONKEY. That donkey had carried many a sack to the mill and never once complained. But now he was old, not too strong anymore, and not fit for such hard work. So the man thought, "Why should I keep feeding him? I'll drive him off, that's what I'll do."

The donkey sensed an ill wind blowing, and left while the going was good. He headed for Bremen. He thought, "I'll become a town musician there."

After he'd walked a little while, he saw a hound sprawled out by the roadside, trying to catch his breath.

"Hey there, Rabbit-Grabber," said the donkey, "why are you panting like that?"

"Ah me," sighed the hound, "I'm old, I'm not so good at hunting anymore. The other day my master shot a partridge. I went for it, I grabbed it, but my teeth are wobbly, and it dropped. My master beat me, so I took off. But now, how will I earn my daily bread?"

"I'll tell you," said the donkey. "I'm going to Bremen to be a town musician. Come along, and be one, too. I'll play the lute, *strum, strum*, and you can beat the drum."

"Good idea," said the hound, and they went on.

Before long they saw a cat sitting by the roadside, looking as gloomy as three days' rain.

"Old Whisker-Washer, why so glum?" asked the donkey.

"Why should I look jolly?" she replied, "I'm aging fast, my teeth are blunt, I'd rather sit by the hearth and purr than chase after mice anymore. My mistress tried to drown me, so I fled. But now where should I go?"

"To Bremen," said the donkey. "You're good at singing serenades. Come with us, we'll all be town musicians."

The cat liked the idea and went along.

Soon the three runaways came to a farm, and on its gate stood a rooster, crowing loud and mournfully.

"You crow as though your heart is breaking," said the donkey. "Redhead, what's the matter?"

"My mistress counted on me to predict the weather. Trying to please her, I always predicted that it would be sunny. But did my mistress thank me? No. She told the cook, 'Kill that old rooster, he'll make good chicken soup.' And so I crow while I still can, before my neck is wrung."

"Cheer up, Redhead," said the donkey, "You have a good strong singing voice. We're going to Bremen to be town musicians. Come with us."

The rooster liked the idea, and all four went on.

But it was far to Bremen. They couldn't get there in one day.

Toward evening they came into a wood. "Let's stay here overnight," the donkey said.

He and the hound lay down under a big tree.

The cat climbed up into the branches.

The cock flew to the very top. He looked around, and spied a dim light gleaming, not too far away. "I think I see a house," he called to his companions.

"Good," said the donkey. "These lodgings here are not so cozy. Let's go there."

"Yes, and I wouldn't mind finding a few bones with bits of meat on them," the hound said.

So they walked and walked in that direction, toward the house in which that light was shining bright.

The donkey, being the biggest, looked in through the window.

The rooster asked, "Old Hee-Haw, what do you see?"

"What do I see? Rough-looking fellows. I think they're robbers. They're sitting at a table laden with food and drink. And they're stuffing their bellies full."

"*Our* bellies could use stuffing, too," the rooster said.

"Yes, if only we could get inside," said the donkey

13

longingly, "But how can we chase those robbers out?"

They put their heads together, and came up with a way:

The donkey stood with his forelegs on the window.

The hound jumped on the donkey's back.

The cat climbed on top of the hound.

The rooster fluttered up and sat on the cat's head.

The donkey lowered his left long ear. That was the signal for the music to start:

Eee aww, bow wow, miaow, miaow, kee-kee-ker-ee-kee! And—SMASH!—the four musicians crashed through the window, and landed amidst shattering, clattering window glass.

"Help! A demon from hell is in our house!" The robbers got so frightened, they jumped up from their chairs, and ran, faster than rabbits, out the door and off into the woods.

The four musicians picked themselves up, sat down at the table, and ate and drank to their hearts' content, until there was nothing left.

Then they put out the light and picked out cozy sleeping places to suit their natures and their needs:

The donkey lay down on a dung heap outside.

The hound, behind the back door.

The cat, on the hearth near the ashes, nice and warm.

The rooster perched high up on the roof beam.

They were tired out from all the walking and commotion, and soon fell sound asleep.

Sometime after midnight the robbers looked back at their house. "The light isn't on, and I don't hear noises coming from there," said the chief. "Maybe we shouldn't have gotten so scared." And he told one of his men, "Go and see what's going on."

The robber went and found everything dark and quiet. He went into the kitchen, saw the cat's eyes glowing, and thought they were two coals. He struck a match, and when he tried to light them up, the cat sprang at his face, spitting and scratching, scaring him out of his wits. He tried to run out through the back door, but the hound leaped up and bit him in the leg. "Ouch, ouch," cried the robber and limped into the yard. When he passed the dung heap, the donkey kicked him good and hard. Just then the rooster on the roof beam awoke, and crowed with all his might, *"Kee-ker-ee-kee!"*

The robber ran faster than he'd ever run, back to the chief and gasped, "An ugly witch sits in the house! She breathed her stinky breath at me, then spat and scratched my face with her sharp fingernails! An ogre with a knife stands by the door, he cut me in the leg! A horrible monster in the yard beat me with a cudgel! Worst of all, up on the roof beam sits a judge, who shouted, "Bring the cree-mee-nal to meee!"

The robbers got so frightened, they never returned to the house.

The four musicians made themselves at home. They never left, and live there even now.

This funny, wise, familiar tale stays fresh just the way the Brothers Grimm retold it. All I invented were new names for the musicians: "Old Hee-Haw," "Whisker-Washer," and "Kee-Ker-Ee-Kee," which is how roosters crow in German.

The Hare and the Hedgehog

THIS TALE HAPPENED ONE Sunday morning before harvest time, just when the buckwheat was in bloom. The sun was up, the sky was bright, the breeze blew softly over the field, the larks sang in the air, and the bees buzzed in the buckwheat blossoms. All creatures were content. The hedgehog's wife was, too.

She stood by her door, stretching her arms out to catch the morning breeze, and gruntingly, squeakily sang a song, no better and no worse than any hedgehog's wife would likely be singing on such a Sunday morning. And while she sang, she got an idea: "I'll let my husband fix breakfast for a change, and I will take a little walk, and see how our turnips are doing."

The turnips grew very close to their house, and they were so used to eating them, that they naturally thought of them as theirs.

She shut the door behind her, and was going around the

18

blackthorn bush where the path to the turnip field began
when she caught sight of Hare. He was out on business
not unlike her own: namely, to see how his cabbages
were doing.

"A friendly good morning, Hare," she called.

Hare thought himself too fine a gentleman, to return
the greeting of a lowly hedgehog's wife. And so he didn't
greet her back, just asked her snootily, "What brings you
out so early?"

"I'm going for a walk," she said.

"For a walk?" Hare laughed. "Can't you think of a
better use for those legs of yours?"

19

Mrs. Hedgehog didn't mind good-natured teasing. But she minded remarks about her legs, which happened to be crooked, nature having made them so. "You think *your* legs are so much better?" she asked angrily.

"I do indeed," said Hare.

"We'll see about that." And she challenged him, "Let's race. I bet I can outrun you."

"With those pathetic legs? Ha ha, that's funny!" Hare

20

laughed even louder. "But you are serious, I can see. Very well. What shall the wager be?"

"One gold ducat and a turnip pie," she replied.

Hare agreed. "Let's shake on it, and start at once."

"No, Hare. I'm not in a big hurry. My stomach is empty. First I'll go home and have a bite of breakfast. I'll meet you here in half an hour."

"Fine with me," said Hare.

The hedgehog wife went home, and this is what she thought: "Hare relies on his long legs, and has a high opinion of himself. But he's a stupid fellow. I'll teach him a thing or two . . ."

When she got home she said, "Husband, come out to the field with me."

"Why? What for?" he asked.

"I bet Hare a ducat and a turnip pie that I can outrun him. And so I shall, but you have to help."

"Outrun Hare? For heaven's sake! What can you be thinking of? Have you lost your mind?"

"Not at all. I know what I'm doing. Please, come with me," she asked him very nicely.

And he did.

Along the way, she told him, "Listen carefully. Here is my plan: This long field will be the race course. Hare will run in one furrow; and I, in the other. We'll start at the top. All *you* need do is hide in a furrow down at this end, and when Hare comes along, stand up and call, "I'm already here!"

She showed him where to hide. Then she went to the starting place.

Hare was already there, and asked, "Now can we begin?"

"Yes."

They each stood in their furrow. Hare counted, "One, two, three, go!" And off they went like a windstorm down the field. But the hedgehog's wife ran only a short distance, then crouched down in her furrow and stayed there quietly.

When Hare came racing to the bottom of the field, the hedgehog husband called, "I'm already here!"

Hare stopped in his tracks, amazed. He naturally thought it was the hedgehog's wife. "But how could that have happened? Something's not right," he thought, and said, "We'd better run the race again."

This time they started at the bottom of the field. One, two, three, and off they ran: Hare, all the way, so fast his ears were flying around his head; but the hedgehog husband ran only three paces, then crouched down in the furrow and hid.

When Hare, running full speed ahead, approached the top of the field, the hedgehog's wife stood up in her furrow and called, "I'm already here!"

"How can this be? We have to do it over," Hare shouted furiously, "Let's run the race again!"

"Fine with me, as often as you like," said the hedgehog's wife.

So Hare ran seventy-three more times, down the field, and up the field, while the hedgehogs hid, now at the bottom, now the top, then called out, "I'm already here!"

But when Hare ran for the seventy-fourth time, he couldn't finish. In the middle of the field he fell down— weak, breathless, all worn out. "I give up! You won!" he gasped.

The hedgehog's wife took the ducat and the turnip pie. By then the hare had fallen asleep, so he didn't see that *two* little hedgehogs walked away on crooked legs and headed for their home.

So this is the story of the hare and hedgehogs' race. And since that Sunday morning, a long, long time ago, no hare has ever ventured to race with a hedgehog again.

The story has two morals: First, no one, regardless how highly he rates himself, should make fun of someone he thinks less of, even if that someone is a hedgehog. And second: If you're looking to get married, and might someday race with a hare, you'd better choose a mate who looks a lot like you.

In other retellings, it's always the hedgehog husband
who masterminds the race, and the wife who does what she's told.
I humbly took the liberty of switching things around.

KING OF THE BIRDS

NE SUNNY MAY MORNING, the birds got together to choose a king. They came flying from fields and forests: the eagle, the bullfinch, the starling, the crow, the hoopoe, the cuckoo, the sparrow, the swallow—I won't try to name them all. Oh, and a plain, grayish bird came, too. He was so little, he didn't even have a name, and no one paid him much attention.

The crow cawed the meeting to order, and this is what the birds agreed: They'd hold a flying contest. And whoever flew highest would be King.

They were trying to decide what the signal to start should be. Just then a frog at the edge of the pond went *"Garoomph!"*

"Contestants, get ready!" cawed the crow.

"Garoomph!" croaked the frog. Up rose the feathered swarm, with *whoosh* and *whirr*.

Before long, the smaller birds got tired, and flew back to the ground.

The bigger ones had more strength, and flew higher. But soon they too returned.

Finally, only the eagle still flew. He soared and circled up so high, he could have pecked out the eyes of the sun. "But why should I fly higher?" he thought to himself. "It's obvious I have won!" And he started to descend.

"Eagle, Eagle, you are King," cheered the birds down on the ground. "No one flies higher than you!"

"Except for me!" said—who? A tiny bird, plain, but also very smart! He'd snuck himself under the eagle's wing, and nestled in the plumage there. It was a soft, warm hiding place, and he'd enjoyed the ride.

Now, as the eagle headed down, out crept that grayish little bird. He felt rested and full of vigor. Up he flew— so high, that he could see God sitting on His throne.

"*I* flew highest!" he exclaimed.

It was true. Not even the eagle could deny it. The

27

birds set a crown on his grayish head—a golden crown. Look! See it shining there? And they proclaimed him King— or rather, Kinglet (on account of his being so small.)

In Germany, where there are no kinglets,
this tale is called Der Zaunkönig
(King of the Fence, meaning wren).

WHEN THE BIRDS AND THE BEASTS WENT TO WAR

EAR AND WOLF WENT walking in the woods one day in summertime. "Brother Wolf, what bird is that who sings so prettily?" asked Bear.

"That is the king of the birds," Wolf replied, "We have to bow to him." And he was right, because it was the kinglet.

"Oh really?" asked Bear, "Can I see his palace? Will you lead me to it?"

"It's not so easy to find," Wolf said. "We'll have to wait until the royal couple returns and guides us there."

Soon the king and his queen came flying to a hole in a tree. They had food in their beaks, and started to feed their young.

Bear wanted to follow. "No," said Wolf, and held him back by the foreleg. "We'd better wait until their majesties fly away again."

And wait they did. When the king and queen were gone Wolf said, "Now you can look."

So Bear looked in the nest. He saw six tiny birds in there. "Some palace!" he scoffed. "It's just a clump of sticks and straws." And he called to the young birds, "You're nothing but puffs of fluff."

"You insult us! We're royal princes and princesses! We'll make you sorry, you will see!" The little birds screeched

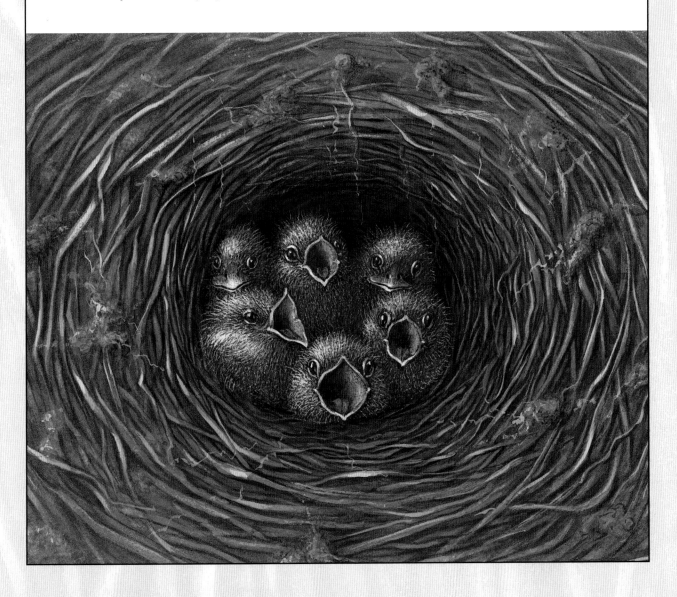

so shrilly, that Bear and Wolf ran away, Bear to his cave, and Wolf to his lair.

When the royal parents returned to the nest with more food in their beaks, the young birds were still angry.

"We don't want any food," they screeched. "Bear was here, insulting us, he called us 'puffs of fluff!' He must apologize, address us by our proper titles, as princes and princesses! We won't eat until he does, even if we have to starve!"

"Bear shall beg your pardons, I shall see to it," their father promised. And he flew to Bear's cave.

He called, "Old Growler, are you in there? Did you insult my children? Then we're at war, you hear? It will be a bloody war, and you'll be very sorry!"

Not until Kinglet was gone did Bear come out of the cave. Then he went to see *his* king, the lion, and told him what had happened.

Lion called his subjects together—the ox, the donkey, deer and doe, and all four-legged beasts that walked and ran and galloped on the earth.

And Kinglet called together all the creatures of the air, not only birds both big and small, but gnats and hornets, wasps and bees, winged insects of every kind.

When they were all assembled, Kinglet sent out spies to discover the enemy's secrets.

One such spy was Gnat. She flew to the wood where the beasts were gathered. She settled herself on a leaf of a branch right above Lion's head, and overheard him say: "Come forward, Fox! You are the slyest of us. Will you be our general and lead us into battle?"

Fox said, "I will. What shall I signal with?"

No one had any idea.

"*I've* got it!" said Fox. "I'll use my fine, long, bushy tail! For it can be seen from near and far. Now here's how we'll proceed: When I raise my tail it means all is well; advance, attack! But if I let it droop, then all is lost; retreat, run for your lives!"

Gnat heard all of this, flew home, and reported to Kinglet.

When the day of battle dawned the four-legged army thundered to the battlefield. Their paw- and hoof-beats caused the earth to tremble. And Kinglet's army came on wings that set the air awhirr.

When the two armies stood facing each other, Kinglet sent out Hornet. Her mission was to sit under Fox's tail and sting for all she was worth.

The first time she stung, it gave Fox a jolt, but he gritted his teeth, and kept his tail up high.

The second time she stung, he let his tail droop, but just a little, and only for a moment.

The third time Hornet stung, the pain was oh so sharp! General Fox couldn't stand it. He yowled. His tail drooped way, way down. He tucked it between his legs. And the beasts, thinking that all was lost, retreated! They ran, ran, ran for their lives.

That was the end of the battle, and of the war!

Their majesties the kinglets flew home to their palace. "Children, be glad! We've won! Now you can eat to your hearts' content!"

"Not yet," the children screeched. "First, Bear must beg our pardons, and call us by our royal titles. We insist!"

36

So Kinglet flew to Bear's cave again, calling, "Old Growler, come out! Make amends to my children, or we'll tear you limb from limb!"

Bear went to the palace. He bowed deeply, and addressed Kinglet's children as princes and princesses. Now their fast was over. They feasted on worms galore, and other avian delights, and everyone made merry until late into the night.

Wouldn't it be wonderful if every war would end so quickly,
with no worse injury to anyone than
what poor Fox endured?

THE WOLF AND THE SEVEN YOUNG KIDS

ONCE THERE WAS A nanny goat. She had seven young kids, and loved them as much as any mother loves her children. One day she called them all to her and said, "Dear children, I have to go into the wood to get food. Be careful while I'm away. Watch out for the wolf. Don't let him in, or he'll eat you up, hide and hair. He's very bad, and very tricky. He often comes disguised. But you can always recognize him by his rough voice and black feet."

"Go, Mother dear, don't worry about us," the eldest kid said. And they all promised, "We'll be careful."

So the nanny goat went on her way.

Before long, someone knocked at the door and called, "Open up, dear little kids, your mother is here and brings you each a present."

But the kids were not fooled. "We won't open the door," they called, "and you are not our mother! She has a soft, and pleasant voice, but your voice is rough. You are the wolf."

So the wolf went to a shop nearby. He bought a big piece of chalk, and chewed it up and swallowed it down, to make his voice not as rough.

Then back he went, knocked at the door, and called, "Open up, dear kids, your mother is here with a present for each of you."

But he had put his black paw on the window sill. The kids saw it, and called, "We won't open the door. Our mother doesn't have black feet, and you do, because you are the wolf."

So the wolf went to a baker and said, "I hurt my foot by bumping it. Kindly spread some dough on it, to help it heal."

The baker did.

Then the wolf said, "Kindly sprinkle some white flour on my dough-covered paw."

"Uh oh," thought the baker, "the wolf wants to trick somebody," and he refused.

But the wolf said, "If you don't do it, I'll eat you up!" The baker did as he was told. He sprinkled flour on the paw and made it look white.

Then the wolf went back to the goats' house and knocked at the door for the third time, calling, "Kids, open up, your dear mother has come home and brings you presents."

"First, show us your paw," one kid called. And another called, "That way we'll know if you're really our mother." So the wolf put his paw on the window sill. They saw that it was white. They opened the door—

And the wolf came in!

The kids were very frightened and tried to hide, quick quick. One got under the table; the second jumped into bed; the third, into the tile stove; the fourth hid in the kitchen; the fifth, in the cupboard; the sixth, under the washbowl; and the seventh squeezed inside the grandfather clock.

The wolf found them in a jiffy. He snapped them up between his jaws and gulped them down, one after the other—all except the seventh kid, the youngest. That one stayed hidden in the clock.

The wolf waddled out, his hunger satisfied. His

stomach felt heavy. So he lay down in the green meadow under a tree and slept.

It wasn't long before the nanny goat came home from the woods. Oh, what a sight she saw!

The door stood wide open. Table, chairs and benches were up-ended. The washbowl was smashed into a dozen pieces. Bedding, sheets and pillows lay on the floor, and featherdown floated in the air.

The nanny goat looked for her children, but they were nowhere to be found! She called each one by name, but none answered. Finally, when she called the youngest, a faint voice cried, "Mother dear, I'm stuck inside the grandfather clock."

She brought him out from there. He told her that the wolf had come and eaten up the others. You can imagine how the mother goat cried about her poor children.

After a while she went outside. The youngest kid went too. When they came to the tree in the meadow, the wolf was snoring so loud that all the branches shook.

The mother goat looked at him from all sides and saw something kicking inside his fat belly. "Dear God," she thought, "oh, can it be that my poor children whom he gulped down are still alive?"

"Quick, run home, bring scissors, needle and thread," she told the youngest kid. He ran and brought them. Then she slit an opening in the monster's belly—and a little kid stuck out his head!

She went on cutting, and all six kids came jumping out, one after the other, alive! And they weren't even hurt, because the wolf had been so greedy, he hadn't stopped

to chew them up, but had swallowed them down whole.

Then there was great rejoicing!

The kids hugged their mother and hopped around as happily as a tailor at his wedding.

"And now, dear children," the mother said, "go find some great big heavy stones, and we'll stuff them in the wolf's belly while he's still asleep."

The seven kids hurried. They brought big, heavy stones, and stuffed them into the wolf's belly, as many as it could hold. Then the mother sewed it up so fast, he didn't notice and didn't even budge.

When he'd finally slept long enough, he got to his feet. And because the stones inside made him thirsty, he headed for the well to drink. But when he got moving the stones banged around, and made loud, rumbling noises. And he grumbled to himself, "What is that rumbling in my belly? It doesn't feel like tasty little goat kids in there. No, it feels like great big, heavy stones!"

When he came to the well, and bent down to the water, trying to drink, the heavy stones pulled him in. And he was gone in an instant!

The seven kids saw all of this, and came running. "The wolf is dead! The wolf is dead!" they sang, and they danced with their dear mother, all around the well.

*In the Grimm Brothers' time this tale was told as a warning
to kids (the human kind) not to let strangers in.*

THE FOX
AND THE GEESE

ONE TIME FOX CAME came to a meadow where a flock of fine, fat geese were sitting.

Fox laughed and said, "I couldn't have come at a better time. Here you all are, and I'm very hungry. I think I'll eat you up."

The geese cackled with fright. They jumped to their feet, they moaned and cried, and pleaded piteously for their lives.

But Fox wouldn't listen and said: "You plead in vain."

But still they went on. Then one goose, a brave one, said, "If we must lose our lives, show us a mercy: Allow us one prayer, so that we don't die with our sins upon us. Then, when we're done, we'll stand in a row so you can easily pick out the fattest of us every time."

Fox said, "That is a pious request. What's more, it makes good sense. Yes, start your prayers. I can wait that long."

So the first goose began a very lenghty prayer, "Ga! Ga! Ga! Ga!" It sounded as though she had no intention of finishing anytime soon. The second goose didn't wait for

46

her turn, instead she too began, "Ga! Ga!" The third and fourth geese followed. Soon the whole flock prayed most devoutly, "Ga! Ga! Ga!" When they all finish, this story will be finished too, but meantime they're still praying, "Ga! Ga! Ga! Ga! Ga! Ga! Ga! Ga! Ga! Ga! Ga! Ga! Ga! . . ."

This sly tale belies the old saying, "All good things must end."
These clever geese go on ga-ga-ing, which goes to show
how helpful prayer can be.

JACOB GRIMM (1785-1863)
WILHELM GRIMM (1786-1859)

Born in Hesse, Germany, just one year apart, Jacob and Wilhelm Grimm were best friends as well as brothers. They played together in their boyhood, and worked together as adults. Jacob was the serious one, not as outgoing and sociable as Wilhelm. In other ways they were alike. They shared high ideals, helped their widowed mother bring up four younger siblings, and did outstandingly at school.

There is an old romantic notion that the Grimm Brothers roamed through the countryside, stopping at humble dwellings, asking peasants to tell them tales, and that they then wrote down these tales with every word in place, straight from their sources' mouths.

In reality their busy careers as lawyers, librarians, government consultants, and university professors left them little time for wandering through fields and woods, dropping in on country folk.

It's true that they collected tales. It's what they're famous for—tales rooted in folklore, which people believed to be a source of great wisdom. However, their sources were almost always city folk—genteel, educated persons like themselves. (One such story teller, Dortchen Wild, eventually married Wilhelm and had three children with him.)

Who ever can transcribe a tale with utter faithfulness to every word? The Grimms reshaped the tales they heard (or, in some cases, got from books). They added things, they took things out, using their own sensibility, which, necessarily, was grounded in the tastes and values of the time—as all retellers do.

—*Doris Orgel*